To Darrell,
who makes everything worth it,
and
Ned, Brett, Bill and Dorothy

and to Neal

Library of Congress Cataloging-in-Publication Data

Julian, Alison, 1945–
   Brave as a bunny can be / written and illustrated by Alison Julian.
      p. cm.
   Summary: A young rabbit, concerned that he is a "scaredy-bunny," sets out to prove his
bravery by leaving his loving family and living on his own.
   ISBN 0-931674-46-8 (alk. paper)
   [1. Rabbits–Fiction. 2. Fear–Fiction. 3. Courage–Fiction. 4. Family–Fiction.] I. Title.

PZ7.J92948 Br 2001
[E]–dc21

                                                                        2001026262

Waldman House Press, Inc.
525 North Third Street
Minneapolis, MN 55401

Brave as a Bunny Can Be

Written and illustrated
by

ALISON JULIAN

Waldman House Press

Minneapolis

Far outside the city, on the edge of a lovely meadow, a family of rabbits lived in a hillside burrow. All of the rabbits were brave except one. Cooper never felt brave at all. When thunder rolled over the meadow, he shook down to the end of his cottony tail. When big brother Bruno told the story about going into the Dark Green place to feast on miner's lettuce

with their sisters Felicity and Celeste, Cooper was so frightened, he started to quiver.

When Bruno said they saw a ferocious fox and barely escaped with their lives, Cooper ran and hid behind his Mother. More than anything Cooper wanted to be brave.

He wanted to be as brave as a bunny can be.

One afternoon, Cooper lingered in the meadow enjoying a tasty brunch.
When he was almost home, he overheard his brother and sisters talking.
  "I feel mean saying this, but he's such a baby, I don't want him around,"
said Celeste.

"He acts like he's scared of everything," said Bruno. "Let's not let him come into the burrow."

"I'd rather not have a scaredy-bunny hanging around here," said Felicity.

Cooper felt his eyes burning, and his heart seemed filled with stones.
They had to be talking about him. He couldn't go home.
They didn't want him around. He didn't fit in.

He turned away sniffling back tears and quietly made his way down the hill. "I will, I will, I WILL learn to be brave," he said to himself with every hop.

When at last he stopped and turned to look back,
he could see the Dark Green place in the distance,
but he could no longer see his home. He was truly
alone for the first time. He started to tremble.

He thought he'd never stop shaking. He started digging to stop his trembling. He began slowly, then worked faster and faster until he was digging harder than he ever had in his life. He dug and dug and then he lined his burrow with timothy grass and his tummy fur.

Cooper lived alone for many weeks,

unaware that every day his family was searching for him.

Every morning he thought up tests of bravery, hoping one day he would feel as brave as a bunny can be, brave enough to return home.

Sleeping alone was brave, he thought.

Living in a new place was brave, too.

Eating alone was brave.

But then, when he thought of the others, especially Mama, his eyes would sting and his tummy would ache, which made him believe he was a scaredy–bunny.

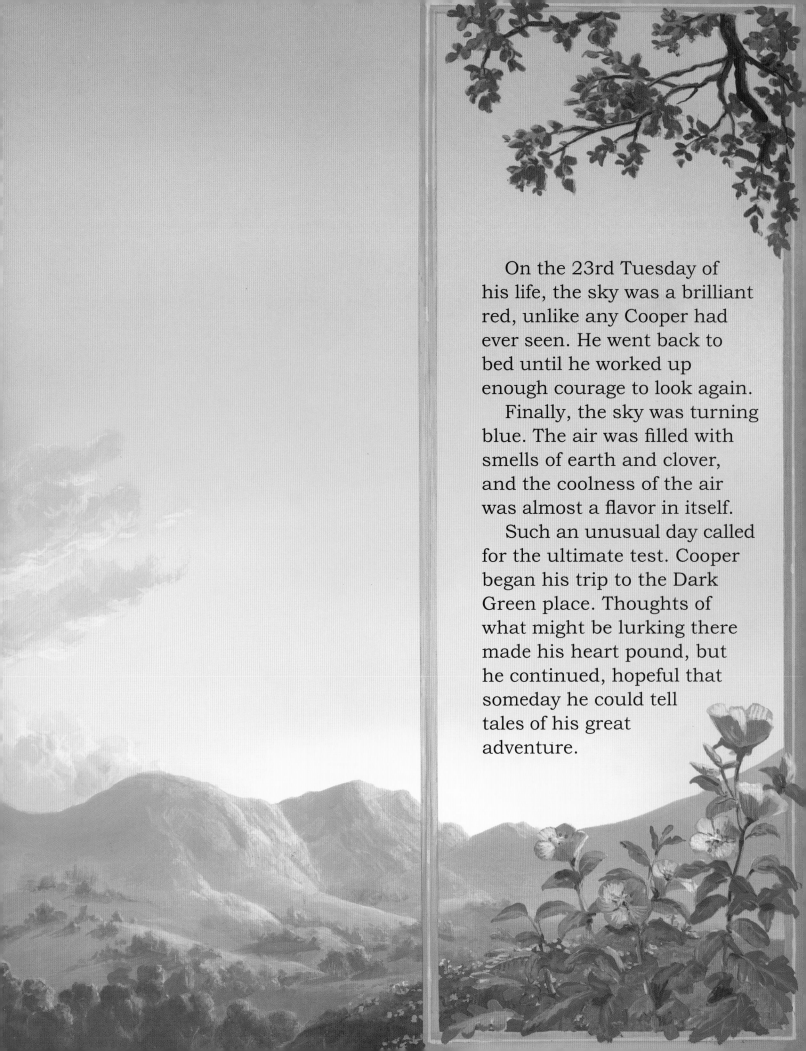

On the 23rd Tuesday of his life, the sky was a brilliant red, unlike any Cooper had ever seen. He went back to bed until he worked up enough courage to look again.

Finally, the sky was turning blue. The air was filled with smells of earth and clover, and the coolness of the air was almost a flavor in itself.

Such an unusual day called for the ultimate test. Cooper began his trip to the Dark Green place. Thoughts of what might be lurking there made his heart pound, but he continued, hopeful that someday he could tell tales of his great adventure.

He lost himself in a fresh patch of clover at the edge of the Dark Green place. And then, past a fallen tree, there it was, the juicy miner's lettuce,

succulent and sweet with its tiny white blossoms.
He hopped over to the lettuce patch and feasted,
not noticing the slowly darkening sky.

Cooper ate until he saw a flash of light. When he looked up, a clap of thunder boomed, and he found himself looking into two copper-colored eyes. A fox!

He held his breath. He didn't blink. Cooper became not a rabbit, but part of the tree behind him. He was trembling inside, but the fox couldn't see that.

The fox stared straight at him when a large drop of water fell onto the fox's nose. PLAP!

The fox looked up and two more drops fell right onto his face.

When the fox blinked, Cooper changed from the tree into the wind. He jumped over the miner's lettuce, ran past the fallen tree, leapt over mossy rocks into the open, and into the rain.

He could hear the fox dash over the rocks behind him.

The rain drops were huge and coming down thick and fast. Blonk! Plomp! Plop! They splashed into Cooper's eyes and soaked his fur down to the skin. The grasses surrendered to the storm and lay flat. Faster the rain came,

until the ground turned all slippery and gooey. Mud, all squishy and cold and heavy, stuck to his paws, but Cooper kept running. Fear made him run toward his home burrow. He felt the fox closing in on him and then an amazing thing happened.

"Charge," he heard Felicity call out. What seemed like an army of rabbits appeared and ran straight for the fox. Cooper skidded to a stop in front of his old home and wanted more than anything to run inside to safety, but he didn't.

He spun around and saw Mama veer to the right, Felicity to the left, and Bruno and Celeste continue straight for the fox.

The confused fox slowed for a moment.

In that second, Bruno jumped out of the fox's reach, but when Celeste

tried to dodge out of the way, she slipped in the mud and skidded closer and closer to the jaws of the snarling fox.

Cooper had no time to think about his fear.

He leaped directly at the fox. The fox jumped into the air and snapped at Cooper. He felt the heat of the fox's breath and heard the sharp teeth snap shut. He felt the bite on his hind leg, but the fox only got a mouth full of muddy fur.

Cooper landed
and watched as
the fox fell and slipped
down the hill, all paws
and mud and tail,
skidding and snarling and
yipping in self-pity. Cooper
stared in disbelief as the
enemy slipped away and he
started feeling…well…brave.

"Hooray," his family cheered.
"Hooray for the bunny who saved the day," cried Felicity.
"Bravo for Cooper, who beat the fox," said Bruno.
"You're the most daring bunny I know," said Celeste. "You saved my life."

Mama hopped up to him. "Thank goodness you're home. We missed you. We've been so worried! But where have you been? And why did you leave?"

"I heard the others talking, two big-moons ago. They said they didn't want a scaredy-bunny like me around."

"Oh, Cooper, we were talking about that little bunny from down the hill," said Felicity. "You know that he's no fun to have around because he's too afraid to try anything."

Cooper lowered his voice so only Mama could hear him. "I was scared almost the whole time I was away, especially when I saw the fox," he said.

Mama nuzzled him, then whispered in his ear, "Don't worry, being scared is part of being brave. The brave part is doing your best, even when you're scared."

Cooper nestled his nose into Mama's fur and it felt so good, he didn't mind that he had been scared. Like Mama said, being scared was part of being brave.

"Now for heaven's sake, clean up," said Felicity. She was right.

He was dreadfully wet and muddy. Mama set to work helping Cooper get his muddy matted fur smooth and silky again.

When they were all clean, Cooper followed his family into the sleepnest. He settled down into its silken fluffiness.

He remembered the scary red sky, the sweet taste of miner's lettuce, the color of the fox's eyes. He thought of the chase, of saving Celeste, and the fox slipping and yipping down the hill. Finally, he savored the chorus of cheers from his family.

He looked around at the others and felt so proud....

…He had lived alone, and survived the Dark Green place.

He outfoxed the fox and saved his sister.

He still felt scared sometimes, but now he knew—he was as brave as a bunny can be.

The rain continued the rest of the day and made the music of tiny little rivers.

Cooper stretched and yawned and took a long sniff. He smelled his home and nothing could have been better. He fit into his family of brave rabbits.

Perfectly.